SLEEPY Time Olie

by William Joyce

ATHENEUM
Books for Young Readers
New York   London   Toronto   Sydney   New Delhi

It's Rolie Polie evening.

The Rolie day is ending.

Sleepy eyes are everywhere—

the moon,

the house,

the rocking chair,

and Olie's Rolie Polie bear.

Rolie Polie evening—
Olie's almost sleeping.
His Rolie days are without care,
especially when Pappy's there
reading in his rocking chair.

It's late enough.
He should be there.
But where is Pappy?
Where oh,
oh where?

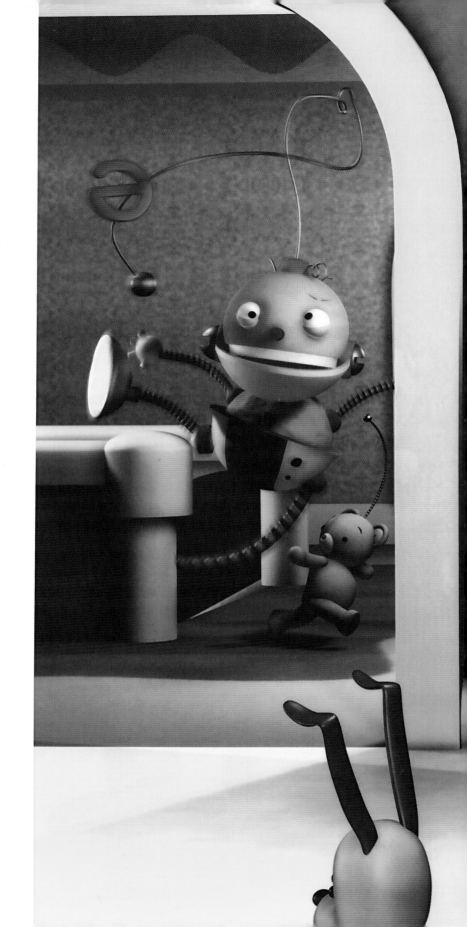

Rolie Polie
evening—
What is all that
squeaking?

Pappy comes in
all unwound.
"I bonked my head.
I just fell down.
I broke my smile.
I can't unfrown.
I might as well
get out of town. . . .

"My heart has lost its swing,
my legs have lost their sway.
My step has not a bit of spring,
my hip has no hooray.
I feel old and all kerploppy—
I'm a walking junk parade.
My cheeks do not feel cheeky.
My red-letter day has grayed."

So he rolled into bed
and that's exactly where he stayed.

But Olie knew just what to do
to make old Pappy feel like new.
"I'll make a super silly ray!"
excitedly said Olie.
"And with it I will save the day
for all things Rolie Polie!"

He grabbed
a goofy this
and a very doofy that,
a hammer
nicknamed Phyllis
and a most peculiar hat.
An extremely funny bone
shaped rather
like a pelvis, and a shot
of Uncle Gizmo
as he danced around
like Elvis . . .

a single Zowie
hopscotch hop,
a book of jokes that
laughed nonstop,
a really, really
loud hiccup
supplied by Spot—
he's some swell pup!

Then Olie burst
into the room
and with his ray
dispelled the gloom.
"I made a Pappy
pick-me-up
to help old Pappy
ungrow-up."

Then Pappy grinned as, deep inside,

his silly gear began to glide.

It tickled every Pappy part,

it ungrew-up his sad old heart.

Up and out young Pappy flew,

feeling happy and brand-new.

They walked on walls, swirled through the air, and danced around in bubbles. If robots spend the day that way, they can't have any troubles.

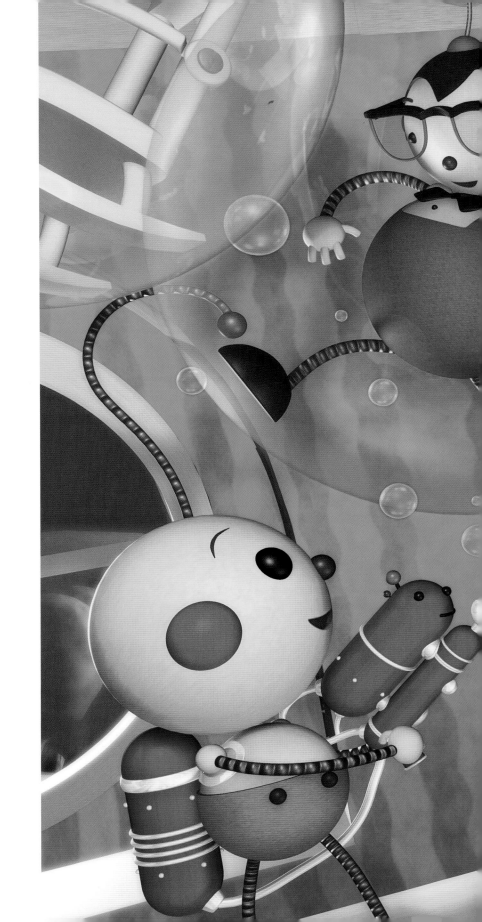

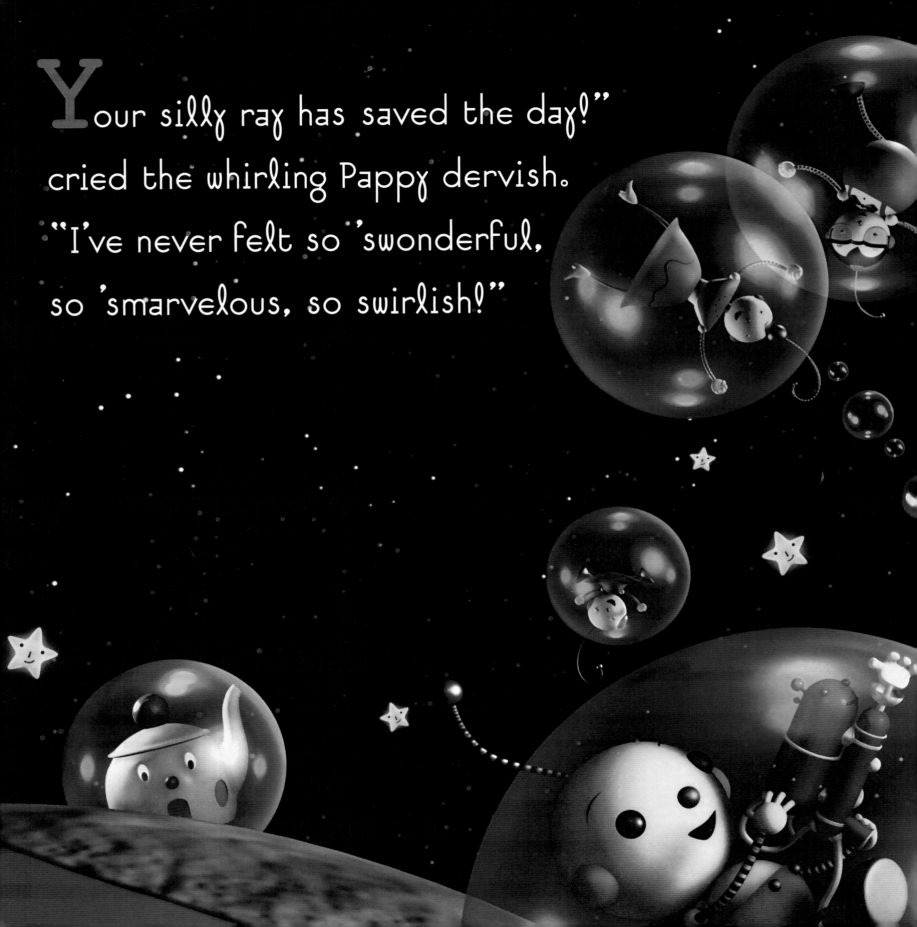

Your silly ray has saved the day!"
cried the whirling Pappy dervish.
"I've never felt so 'swonderful,
so 'smarvelous, so swirlish!"

The Rolie moon and stars and sun
joined in the happy Pappy fun.
And when the Polie fun was done,
they bubbled homeward one by one.

Rolie Polie evening—
the house will soon be sleeping.

Jammies on for all robots.

They're moving slow, they're yawning lots,
they're wearing Rolie polka dots.

Rolie Polie evening—
Olie's day is ending.
Happy Pappy, warm and wise,
reads lullabies and hushabies
beneath the sleepy Rolie skies.

Rolie Polie evening—
Olie now is sleeping.
His dreams are filled
with silly rays
and hip hoorays
and happy
Pappy holidays.
All Rolie dreams
are without care,
especially if
Pappy's there.

Rolie Polie evening—
everything is sleeping—
the moon,
the house,
the rocking chair....

Everything . . .

everywhere...

is sleeping now

without a care.

For
Pop Pops

Gargantuan
kudos to the most
righteous robo-dudes Jordan
Thistlewood and Gavin Boyle; Susie
Grondin, the shimmering queen of getting
things done; the grand high Pamatola, Pam Lehn;
the Nelvana 3D group for the reuse of their models;
Shannon Gilley, Darin Bristow, and Paul Cieniuch,
the mystery computer dudes; twin czarinas of design
and production Alicia Mikles and Ruiko Tokunaga;
Tamar Brazis, my own personal Pandora; Emily,
Trish, and Katie, the foxy crime-fighting
trio; and Laura Geringer, raven-
haired warrior goddess of
publishing.

atheneum

ATHENEUM BOOKS FOR YOUNG READERS
An imprint of Simon & Schuster Children's Publishing Division
1230 Avenue of the Americas, New York, New York 10020
Text copyright © 2001 by William Joyce • Illustrations copyright © 2001 by Nelvana Limited.
All rights reserved. Artwork reprinted by permission of Nelvana Limited. • All rights reserved,
including the right of reproduction in whole or in part in any form. • ATHENEUM BOOKS FOR YOUNG
READERS is a registered trademark of Simon & Schuster, Inc. Atheneum logo is a trademark of Simon &
Schuster, Inc. • For information about special discounts for bulk purchases, please contact Simon & Schuster
Special Sales at 1-866-506-1949 or business@simonandschuster.com. • The Simon & Schuster Speakers Bureau
can bring authors to your live event. For more information or to book an event, contact the Simon & Schuster
Speakers Bureau at 1-866-248-3049 or visit our website at www.simonspeakers.com. • Book design by Alicia Mikles •
The text for this book was set in Rollie Suburban. • The illustrations for this book were digitally rendered. •
Manufactured in China • 0118 SCP • First Atheneum Books for Young Readers Edition • 10 9 8 7 6 5 4 3 2 1
Library of Congress Cataloging-in-Publication Data • Names: Joyce, William, 1957– author. • Title: Sleepy time Olie /
William Joyce. • Description: First edition. | New York : Atheneum Books for Young Readers, [2017] |
Originally published by Laura Geringer Books/HarperCollins Publishers in 2001. | Summary: When Pappy
bumps his head before bedtime, Olie cheers him up by inventing a super silly ray, and then they both
become happy, sleepy robots. • Identifiers: LCCN 2016034992 | ISBN 9781481489638
(hardcover : alk. paper) | ISBN 9781481489645 (eBook : alk. paper) • Subjects: |
CYAC: Stories in rhyme. | Robots—Fiction. | Inventions—Fiction. | Bedtime—Fiction.
Classification: LCC PZ8.3.J835 Sl 2017 | DDC [E]—dc23
LC record available at
https://lccn.loc.gov/2016034992